KAREN
KINGSBURY
#1 *NEW YORK TIMES*
Bestselling Author and NFL Quarterback
ALEX SMITH

GO AHEAD and DREAM

ILLUSTRATED BY GREG BANNING

HARPER
An Imprint of HarperCollinsPublishers

Published in association with the literary agency of Alive Communications, Inc., 7680 Goddard Street, Suite 200, Colorado Springs, Colorado 80920, www.alivecommunications.com.
Go Ahead and Dream
Text copyright © 2013 by Karen Kingsbury and Alex Smith
Illustrations copyright © 2013 by Greg Banning
Manufactured in China.

Library of Congress Cataloging-in-Publication Data
Kingsbury, Karen.
Go ahead and dream / by *New York Times* bestselling author Karen Kingsbury and NFL quarterback Alex Smith ; illustrated by Greg Banning. — 1st ed.
    p.   cm.
Summary: A beloved grandfather's special song helps inspire two boys to pursue their improbable dreams of becoming a professional football player and an airline pilot. Based on a true story.
ISBN 978-0-06-168625-2 (trade bdg.)
[1. Grandfathers—Fiction. 2. Perseverance (Ethics)—Fiction. 3. Conduct of life—Fiction. 4. Smith, Alex, 1984—Childhood and youth—Fiction.] I. Smith, Alex, 1984– II. Banning, Greg, ill. III. Title.
PZ7.K6117Go 2013   2010015907
[E]—dc22   CIP
                                                                                AC

E KiN   H/LC   12/18/13

Typography by Jeanne L. Hogle
13 14 15 16 17   SCP   10 9 8 7 6 5 4 3 2 1
❖
First Edition

Dedicated to:
Donald, my Prince Charming,
Kelsey, my precious princess,
Tyler, my forever song,
Sean, my happy sunbeam,
Josh, my strong and kind son,
EJ, my chosen one,
Austin, my miracle boy,
And to God Almighty, who has—for now—blessed me with these.
—K.K.

For Leo
—G.B.

When practice was over, quarterback Alex Smith jogged off the San Francisco 49ers field and headed for the locker room. The season would begin in a few weeks, but first he was going back to San Diego. He couldn't wait to see his family and spend a little time with his best friend, Bobby.

Two hours later Alex was on a plane headed home.

His dream of being an NFL quarterback had come true. But it was never easy. And as the plane lifted off, Alex closed his eyes and drifted back in time, back to the beginning.

Suddenly he was in first grade again, hearing the teacher say, "Draw a picture of what you want to be when you grow up."

Alex wanted to be a football player. As he started to draw, he asked his friend Bobby, "What about you?"

Bobby shrugged. "I want to be a pilot, but I don't know. It takes training, and training costs more than shoes."

Bobby's shoes had a hole at the toe. Bobby was a foster child, which meant he didn't live with his mom and dad the way Alex did. He lived with foster parents, different ones all the time. As much as he could, he hung out at Alex's house.

When the teacher saw Alex's picture, she frowned. "You're a smart boy, Alex. You should think about being a doctor or an astronaut." Then she smiled at Bobby's picture. "You'd be a great pilot," she said.

Alex felt his shoulders sink a little. Being a football player was his dream, but maybe it was the wrong dream.

After school, Alex's grandpa picked up the boys because Bobby was spending the night at Alex's house. Grandpa was one of their favorite people in the whole world.

"I want to play football when I grow up," Alex told him. "But our teacher said maybe I should be a doctor."

"I want to be a pilot," Bobby said. "But training costs too much."

Grandpa stroked his chin, and his eyes began to twinkle. "Those are dreams, my boys. I have a little song about dreams. It goes like this."

Go ahead and dream,
However big it seems.
Work hard, Believe,
And don't give up.
Yes, go ahead and dream.

In fifth grade, the kids played kickball at every recess. One by one the other guys got picked for teams, but Alex was always picked last.

Bobby usually had to stay inside because he'd failed one test or another. He almost never thought about being a pilot.

Alex's dream hadn't changed. He still wanted to play football in college and then in the NFL. But how could that happen if he couldn't do better than last pick at recess?

One night Alex's mom asked Bobby about his math test.

Bobby frowned. "What's the point of wanting to be a pilot?" he said. "Foster kids aren't good students, anyway."

Alex grumbled, "I got picked last for kickball again."

But Grandpa smiled a big smile. "Work hard," he said. "And never, ever give up." Then he cleared his scratchy voice and began to sing:

Go ahead and dream,
However big it seems.
Work hard, Believe,
And don't give up.
Yes, go ahead and dream.

After that, the boys worked hard every day. Two weeks later at recess, Alex played his best kickball game ever.

And when Bobby took his test over, he got a B.

More years passed, and Alex was in seventh grade playing the biggest baseball game of his whole life. Everyone came to watch—his mom, his dad, his uncles and cousins, and Bobby. Of course Grandpa was there, because Grandpa was always there. But Alex was sitting on the bench, too short and slow to get in the game.

When the coach didn't call on him for the last inning that day, Alex hung his head. Maybe his dream of playing football wasn't a good one after all.

As he walked out to face his family, he noticed Bobby had been crying.

"Bobby's foster parents can't keep him anymore," Grandpa said. "Since he hasn't been adopted, he has to live in a group home."

Grandpa looked at both boys. "Sometimes life doesn't go the way you want it to," he said. "When that happens, you have two choices. You can give up, or you can try harder."

Bobby still looked sad, but he gave Grandpa a crooked smile. "Like that song you always sing."

"Exactly," Grandpa said. And once again, in his scratchy voice, he began to sing.

Go ahead and dream,
However big it seems.
Work hard, Believe,
And don't give up.
Yes, go ahead and dream.

And Grandpa's song helped.

Alex was in the middle of his high school chemistry class when his teacher called him up front and whispered, "Your dad is in the principal's office. He needs to see you."

Alex opened the principal's door and saw his dad. He saw Bobby, too. And that was when Alex's dad told them the news.

Grandpa had gone to heaven.

They had a service for Grandpa that weekend. Alex and Bobby
both felt lost and confused.

Later that week some of Alex's friends made a plan to skip school. It wasn't the way Grandpa taught him, but Grandpa was gone. Alex felt like his dreams didn't matter anymore.

Bobby spotted him leaving with the guys. "You belong in school," he said. "You want to play college football, remember?"

Alex stared at the ground. "I don't know. Maybe not anymore."

Bobby got mad. "Your grandpa taught us to hold on to our dreams and to keep trying." Bobby grabbed Alex's arm. "You and I are going to class, and then we're going to practice," he said.

A happy feeling spread through Alex, because Bobby was his real friend. Real friends help each other with their dreams.

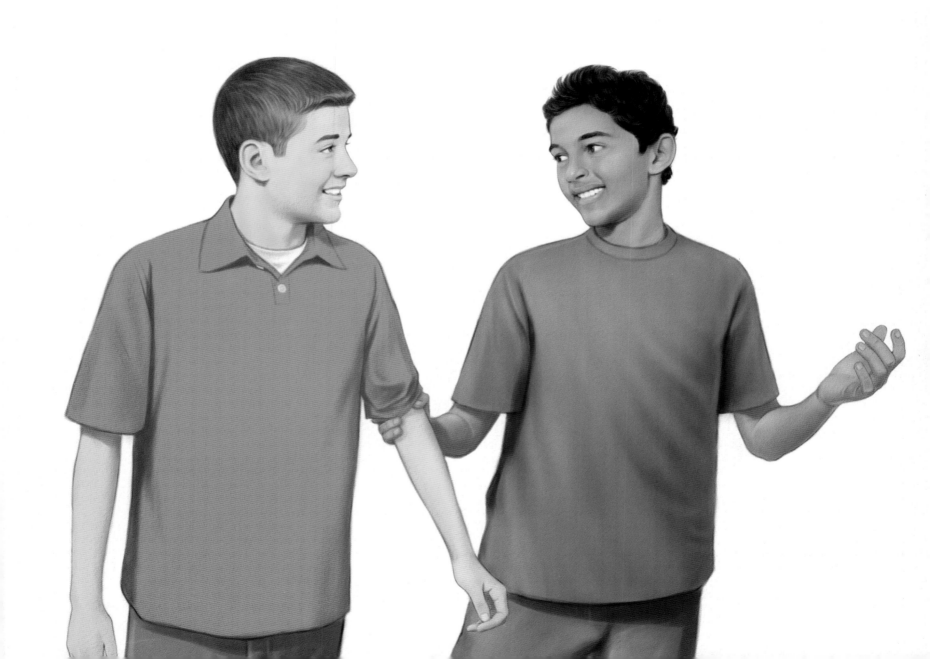

After high school, Alex played football at the University of Utah. He was a
finalist for the Heisman Trophy and the top pick in the first round of the NFL
draft. Bobby still struggled, but he found a way to attend pilot training school.

Alex opened his eyes as the plane's wheels touched the ground. He was the last passenger to leave the aircraft. When he got to the cockpit, he stopped and gave Bobby a big hug. "You look great in a pilot's uniform," Alex said. "You ready?"

"Ready," Bobby said, grabbing his suitcase. "I can't wait to see your family."

Alex grinned. "They can't wait to see you."

As the two friends headed off the plane, Alex had the feeling that somewhere up in heaven, Grandpa was smiling, and maybe he was even singing a little song.

Go ahead and dream,
However big it seems.
Work hard, Believe,
And don't give up.
Yes, go ahead and dream.

Dear Readers,

My dad was bigger than life, a happy man whose booming voice was rich with enthusiasm. He believed in God, his family, and his country . . . and he believed in the importance of following a dream.

When I was growing up, my dad was my biggest fan. I would write a short story or a poem, take it to him, and watch while he read it. His eyes would sparkle, and as he came to the end of the piece he would look at me—all the conviction and belief shining in his expression.

"Karen . . . this is wonderful!" His smile would fill his face. "One day the whole world will know what a tremendously talented writer you are."

As I grew into my later teenage years, the dream began to form. I wanted to be a novelist, but as it is for most kids, there were a number of obstacles in my way. I had no connections and knew no other published authors, and the seemingly insurmountable odds of ever getting published loomed like a mountain no high school girl could ever conquer.

But again my dad had the answer.

"You need to believe," he would tell me. "Someone has to be the next bestselling author, and it might as well be you."

Those few words became an anchor, a reason to believe that among the plans God had for me were certainly plans that I would someday be published. When the day came for my first novel to be released, my dad pulled me aside and smiled at me, tears welling in his eyes. "Congratulations, Karen. I always believed in your dreams . . . someday you'll do the same for your children."

And so I have done just that. My husband and I have always encouraged our daughter and five sons to follow their dreams. Of course, it's important to focus on the other aspects of having a big dream—hard work, persistence, and faith that can move mountains. We work on that as well.

Hard work and the power of having a dream came into play again when I had the privilege of meeting NFL quarterback Alex Smith. He was having one of the best games of his life as a San Francisco 49er. After the game my family met up with his, back at his house. There we took a few minutes to talk about dreams. "My parents always believed in me," Alex told me. He went on to explain that not only his mom and dad but also his grandfather had played a significant role in encouraging his dreams. "I'd like to write a children's book one day helping kids and families understand the importance of holding on to a dream . . . and working hard enough to accomplish it."

With that, the idea for *Go Ahead and Dream* was born.

It is my prayer that as you share this book with your children you will allow time for discussion, time to imagine the big goals ahead. Then you can begin the journey to seeing them come true. Enjoy these days. There is no time like the present to share special moments with your little ones and to help them go ahead and dream.

The way I did when I was growing up.

—KAREN KINGSBURY